Aunt Martha and the Golden Coin

AN AUNT MARTHA STORY
By Anita Rodriguez

Clarkson Potter/Publishers
New York

In the heart of the big city there lived an old woman whose name was Aunt Martha. Aunt Martha was an unusual woman who, it was rumored, possessed magical powers. For a start, she could foretell the weather correctly, and she had a charming way with children and cats. And no one ever attempted to break into her apartment even though it was on the first floor — and that was very unusual for that part of the city.

Although Aunt Martha lived alone, she was never lonely. She always had company, especially the young children in the neighborhood. Often they would come to her house for cookies and stories.

One afternoon, when Mark, Jerry, and Lisa were visiting, Aunt Martha said, "Children, sit down now. I am going to tell you a story about a little girl named Martha."

The children gathered around her, and Aunt Martha began.

A long time ago, when I was a very little girl, I lived far, far away—way down South. We lived on a small farm right next to a huge swamp where my brothers and I used to play. One day when I was out playing, an amazing thing happened.

I noticed a very shiny object hidden in the tall grass. As I approached cautiously, it seemed to grow brighter and brighter. You can imagine my surprise when I picked it up. It was a golden coin with inscriptions in a foreign language on one side, and on the other, a picture of a pyramid.

As I held it in my palm, the golden coin seemed to grow warmer and warmer, and the more I studied it, the hotter it grew until it seemed to burst into flames in my hand. But as I held it, peace filled my heart and all fear left me. I felt strangely comforted as I made my way home through the swamp.

As I was walking down the path, I heard a noise in the underbrush. It was a huge crocodile! I reacted instinctively, squeezing the coin in my hand. Much to my startled surprise, a brilliant flame exploded from the coin and stopped the crocodile in his tracks. He trembled with fright! Then he slithered away as fast as he could and disappeared into the swamp.

When I arrived home, I immediately told my mother about my strange experience. My father examined the coin and concluded that it must have come from Ethiopia, a country in Africa. It was very old and perhaps had been lost by pirates to be discovered by me, Martha, many, many years later.

My father considered it to be very valuable, so my mother hid it on our farm until I was a grown woman.

When I grew up I decided to move up North. My mother gave me the golden coin.

"Keep this with you always, my daughter," she advised. "May you be protected from all harm and always be blessed."

So I took the golden coin and my cat with me. That cat was this cat's great-great-great-grandmother. I came to this big city and I've been here ever since.

"Do you still have the golden coin?" asked Mark.

"Can we see it?" begged Jerry.

"Yes, please," said Lisa.

"Children, that's my secret," said Aunt Martha, smiling.

After the children had gone home, Aunt Martha settled down in her rocking chair to do her knitting. Suddenly she heard a sound in the other room. She quickly got up and turned out the light.

Looking into the room, she saw a strange man outside her window. The man was breaking in! Aunt Martha reached into her pocket and took out the golden coin.

She quickly squeezed the golden coin. It grew hot in her hand and a terrible flame shot out and knocked the intruder down. He was so startled that he let out a loud cry and dropped his gun. Still yelling, he ran off into the night.

Once more, all was at peace in Aunt Martha's apartment. And her secret was still a secret. After all, secrets are not to be told, are they? But the puzzle still remains.

Did Aunt Martha really possess special powers? Was the mysterious coin really from Ethiopia? Was it really endowed with supernatural energies?

Or was her special power the faith in her heart—the faith of an unusual woman who lived in the heart of the big city.

Published by Clarkson N. Potter, Inc., 201 East 50th Street, New York, New York 10022.
Member of the Crown Publishing Group.

Random House, Inc. New York, Toronto, London, Sydney, Auckland

CLARKSON N. POTTER, POTTER, and colophon are trademarks of Clarkson N. Potter, Inc.

Manufactured in Hong Kong

Design by Howard Klein

Library of Congress Cataloging-in-Publication Data

Rodriguez, Anita.
Aunt Martha and the golden coin: an Aunt Martha story / by Anita Rodriguez.
p. cm.

Summary: After telling the neighborhood children about a magical coin she
had found as a child living in the South, Aunt Martha uses the coin's power
again to scare away a burglar.
[1. Afro-Americans—Fiction. 2. Magic—Fiction.] I. Title
PZ7.R6188Au 1993   92-73146
[E]—dc20   CIP
                                                                    AC

ISBN 0-517-59337-8
GLB 0-517-59358-6

10 9 8 7 6 5 4 3 2 1
First Edition